HERMAN BANG
The Four Devils

Contents

A VERY SHORT INTRODUCTION	1
ONE	2
TWO	8
THREE	14
FOUR	18
FIVE	23
SIX	26
SEVEN	32
EIGHT	35
NINE	40
TEN	44
ELEVEN	48
TWELVE	52
THIRTEEN	56
VERY SHORT CLASSICS	60

A VERY SHORT INTRODUCTION

Herman Bang was born in 1857 on the small Danish island of Als. He published his first novel, *Haabløse Slægter (Families Without Hope)*, in 1880. Its subject matter, a man who has an affair with an older women, was considered obscene and the book was subsequently banned.

After spending some years travelling he settled in Copenhagen where he wrote a number of acclaimed novels, making him one of the leading Scandinavian writers of his age and winning the friendship and admiration of many contemporaries, including Henrik Ibsen.

However, as a homosexual he was the victim of smear campaigns and became more and more isolated in the Danish literary world. Nonetheless, he continued to write and enjoyed success as a journalist and novelist and was in high demand around the world as a lecturer. It was during a lecture tour of the United States in 1912 that he was taken ill on a train and died in Ogden, Utah at the age of 54.

ONE

The director's bell rang. Gradually the people drifted into their seats, while the trampling in the balcony, the chatter in the orchestra, and the shouts of the boys who sold oranges almost drowned out the music; and, at last, even the blasé individuals in the boxes settled down in expectation.

The next number was *Quatre Diables*, or *The Four Devils*. The net was stretched in readiness. Fritz and Adolf dashed out of their dressing room into the performers' lobby, and hurried along the passage, their grey cloaks flapping about their legs. They knocked at a door and called, "Aimée and Louise!"

Both sisters were waiting. They too were in a state of feverish excitement, wrapped in long white evening capes which enveloped them completely. Their maid, her felt hat stuck on askew, kept shrieking hoarsely, as she flew aimlessly around, carrying arm rouge and powdered resin.

"Come girls," called Adolf, "It's time." But for another moment they all ran aimlessly about, seized by the fever that attacks all trapeze artists, once they feel the tights on their legs.

The maid was making the most noise.

Aimée alone kept her composure, calmly extending her arms, from the depths of voluminous sleeves, towards Fritz. And quickly, without glancing at her face or speaking a word, he mechanically rubbed the powder puff up and down her outstretched arms, – as he always did.

"Come on," cried Adolf again.

They all ran out, hand in hand, and waited at the entrance, listening from without for the first strains of *The Love Waltz* to which they worked. It began:

> *Amour, amour,*
> *Oh, bel oiseau,*
> *Chante, chante,*
> *Chante toujours.*

Fritz and Adolf threw off their cloaks, and stood forth, radiant in suits of a pink so delicate that it seemed almost white. Their bodies actually appeared naked: every muscle showed.

The music ceased.

Meanwhile in the stable all was still and deserted except for a few attendants occupied in examining the feed bins. They allowed nothing to disturb them in their task of lifting, and suspiciously inspecting, the heavy receptacles.

The melody began again, and The Four Devils entered the ring.

The applause sounded in their ears like a vague roar, and they could not distinguish a face. Every fibre of their bodies seemed aquiver with exertion.

Then Adolf and Fritz quickly unclasped the heavy cloaks for Louise and Aimée; the wraps slipped to the sand and straightway hundreds of opera-glasses were focussed on the girls. They, too, appeared naked in their black tights, like two negresses with white faces.

The four swung themselves into the net and began to work. Nude they all seemed, as they flew to and fro between the swings, with their bars of shining brass. They embraced, caught one another, and encouraged each other with mutual cheers. It seemed as if the black and white bodies were passionately entwined, only to fall apart once more in their seductive nudeness.

And the *Love Waltz* with its sleepily languishing rhythm went on and on; the women's hair, when they flew, fluttered about their black bodies, enveloping them like shining satin cloaks.

They went on and on, working above each other. Adolf and Louise were above the others. The applause reached them in a confused murmur, while the performers in their boxes, among them the still excited maid with her rose-wreathed hat more crazily askew than before, kept their glasses glued on the Devils. These four were known throughout the circus world for their daring.

"Au, au, their hips are quite free."

"The trick, you see, is to have the thighs exposed." These exclamations came from the artists' box.

The stout première equestrienne of The Knights of the Sixteenth Century, Mademoiselle Rosa, laid her glasses heavily to one side. "No, they are not wearing a sign of a corset," she sighed, sweating at every pore, under her own heavy armour.

They continued to work. The electric lights alternated from blue to yellow, as the bodies flew through the air.

Fritz gave a cry as, hanging by his feet, he caught Aimée in his arms. Then they rested, sitting side by side on the trapeze.

They heard Louise and Adolf calling to each other up above; Aimée, with labouring breath, commented on Louise's work:

"Voyez donc, oyez," she cried, as Adolf caught Louise on his legs.

But Fritz made no reply. As he wiped his hands on the little square of cloth that he kept for that purpose, his eyes were glued on the tier of boxes that glowed and swayed far below them like the border of a many-coloured flower-bed.

Suddenly, Aimée, too, grew silent, and stared in the same direction, until, with an obvious effort at detachment, he remarked:

"It's our turn now," and she recalled herself with a jerk.

Again they dried their hands on the cambric, and threw themselves forward, hanging by their arms, as if to try the strength of their biceps. Then back into place again. With their souls in their eyes, they measured the distance between the trapezes. Suddenly both cried:

"Du courage!"

And Fritz flew backwards to the farthest trapeze while Louise and Adolf emitted a long sustained cry, like one who encourages an animal.

> *Amour, amour,*
> *Oh, bel oiseau,*
> *Chante, chante,*
> *Chante toujours.*

Their big act began. They took off backwards, flew past each other with hoarse cries, and reached the distant goal. With another shout, they repeated this. Then, as Louise and Adolf revolved on their swings like wheels endowed with perpetual motion, there fell from the very top of the rotunda a rain of glittering dust that sifted slowly downward, glowing in the pure white flood of the calcium lights. For a moment, the Devils seemed to fly through a shimmering cloud of gold, while the settling dust bespangled their nudity with thousands of golden specks.

Suddenly, one after the other, they shot head-first through the glittering mist into the net – and the music stopped.

In sudden confusion, they leaned on each other as if they had become dizzy. Only after they had answered a number of curtain calls did the applause begin to subside.

Moaning, they ran into their dressing rooms; Adolf and Fritz threw themselves flat on a mattress that lay on the floor, and rolled themselves up in blankets. There they rested a while, almost unconscious. At last they got up and changed their clothes. Adolf looked sharply from his own reflection to Fritz, who was putting on a groom's coat.

"Going on duty?" he inquired.

Fritz answered crossly: "The manager asked me to."

He joined the others who were keeping watch at the stables, and like him, were resting their exhausted bodies against the wall...

After the performance, the troupe gathered in the restaurant. The Devils sat, mute like the others, at a private table. A few of the guests were playing cards, but quite silently. Not a sound, but the clink of the coins as they were pushed across the table. Two waiters stood in front of the buffet, and stared dully at all these silent people, sitting stupidly along the wall, with outstretched legs, and nerveless, dangling arms. The waiters began to turn down the gas.

Adolf laid some money beside one of the bed glasses and got up. "Come on," he said, "let's go." The other three followed.

The streets were quiet; not a sound but their own footsteps, as they walked along two by two, just as they worked. Having reached their boarding place, they parted in the dark entry of the first floor with a soft "Good night."

Aimée waited on the dark landing, until Fritz and Adolf had reached the second floor, and closed the door behind them. Then she joined her sister, and the two girls undressed without saying a word. But, once in bed, Louise began to chat about the work of the others, about the people in the boxes and the regular habitués, for she knew all their faces. Aimée continued to sit, half undressed on the edge of the bed without moving, while Louise's chatter became more and more fragmentary, until she finally fell asleep. A little later, she awoke, and sat up with a start. Aimée was still sitting beside her, in the same position.

"Aren't you *ever* coming to bed?" asked Louise.

Aimée quickly turned out the light. "Right away," she said, and got up. But even in bed she could not sleep. One thing kept going through her mind: that Fritz's eyes never met hers any more when he powdered her arms.

Fritz and Adolf were also in bed, but Fritz tossed about like a man on the rack: Was that meant for him? And what did she want of him, that woman in the box? Did she want anything? Why, then, must she stare at him so persistently? Why brush by him so closely? What did it all mean?

He thought of nothing but this woman. From morning till night, of nothing but her, just her. He felt like an animal in a cage; always the same question kept revolving in his head: what of this woman in the box? He sensed the fragrance of her clothing, as he did whenever she came down and brushed by him, as he stood waiting in his groom's livery.

But was all this really meant to him? What did she want? He continued to toss painfully to and fro, repeating into the darkness, as if it fascinated him, the phrase, *femme du monde!* And the same question surged over him anew. Was it meant to him? Was it meant to him?

Aimée had got up again. Silently, she crept across the room. In the dark, her fingers groped for the rosary in the bureau drawer; they touched it. The house was still so still…

TWO

The devils had been working. In the dressing room, Adolf was scolding because Fritz, so he insisted, had ruined their contract through his everlasting services as groom, for the Devils were exempted from this.

But Fritz had not a word to reply. Every evening, he donned the livery, and taking his post beside the box entrance, waited for the "Lady of the Box" to come out, leaning on her husband's arm. She often sat during the whole of the last act in the stable; and Fritz always followed her. She spoke to the attendants, patted the horses, or read aloud the names affixed to the stalls. Fritz followed her, but to him she never addressed a word.

It was all for his benefit – ah, he knew it well; through 1000 little gestures – the straightening of her back, the movement of her arm, the glance of her eye, she showed that they were destined for one another. They seemed actually to touch, though each took care to keep the distance that separated them. In spite of it, they felt close to each other; it was as if some indescribable impulse had caught them in a double coil that held them both bound. She changed her place, to read the inscription on a new stall. Fritz followed. She laughed, walked on, but returned to pat the dogs. Fritz followed, followed, wherever she led.

TWO

He pretended not to see her. But his eyes rested on the hem of her dress and on her extended hand with the look of a wild beast that is being broken, a look full of lowering hate, because the creature feels his impotence.

One evening she approached him; her husband had walked on a little. He started at her softly breathed question: "Are you afraid of me?"

He hesitated a moment. "I don't know," he answered. His voice was hoarse and harsh. She could not reply. Seized by a sudden fear that sobered her, she realised all that those burning looks conveyed. She turned, and with a short laugh that offended her own tears, walked rapidly away.

On the next evening, Fritz did not go to the stalls. He had determined to avoid her, firmly resolved not to see her again. He felt that engulfing fear of women, which most circus performers have, as lurking foes ready to work on their ruination, mysterious enemies who lie in wait, and are only born to work havoc with a man's strength. And if, carried on the tide of an irresistible impulse, he ever should surrender, this would be with a sort of desperate self-renunciation a vengeful hatred of the woman, who was taking from him a part of his body, robbing him of his strength, his priceless stock-in-trade, his sole means of existence.

But this woman in the box was doubly dangerous, since she was a stranger, and not one of his own kind. What did she want of him? The very thought of her tortured his brain, which was not accustomed to thinking. He watched with apprehension every movement, feeling that she would do him some great, mysterious wrong. Well he knew that there was no escape.

He would not see her again, positively not. It was easy to keep his vow, for she no longer came; not for two days, not three.

On the fourth, Fritz again donned his livery. But she did not appear, either on that evening or the following. All day long, he thought in fear, "If she should come," and in the evening came a dull anger, a brutal, inner rage, because she was not there.

So she had made a fool of him, lured him on, and then cast him off. So that was the kind of woman she was! But he would have revenge, he would find her…

He visualised it all; how he would rain blows upon her, kick and maltreat her, until she arrived and lay half dead – she, that female! At night he lay for hours in silent wrath. And his desire took root during those first sleepless nights, took root in his despair, that he had never lain sleepless before.

Then at last, on the ninth day, she came. From the trapeze he caught sight of her face – he seemed to be looking through the eyes of another – and with a sudden jerk, in boyish exuberance, he launched his magnificent slender body, swinging by his taut arms, out into the air. His face was lighted by a brilliant smile, as he pulled himself up.

> *Amour, amour,*
> *Oh, bel oiseau,*
> *Chante, chante,*
> *Chante toujours.*

Lightly swaying his head in time to the waltz, he seized Aimée's hand gladly and joyfully, for the first time in a week, and called loudly to her, "Enfin, du courage!" It sounded like a shout of triumph. Yet afterwards, when he entered the stalls in his uniform, and found *her* there, he was again stricken dumb; he felt hostile and fixed upon her the same look of hatred that had not dared to meet her eyes before. But in the restaurant, after the performance, he suddenly grew animated, almost reckless.

He laughed loudly, and performed all sorts of tricks. He

juggled cups and steins, and even balanced his high silk hat on the tip of his cane. The other artists were captivated by his high spirits. The clown, Tom, fetched his accordion and played lustily, stalking over the chairs with his long legs.

This excitement ensued. Everybody did tricks. Mr Fillis balanced a huge paper bag on his nose, and two or three clowns cackled, as if they were in a chicken yard. Fritz screamed loudest of all. Having jumped upon a table, he juggled two glass globes that he had unscrewed from the chandelier, and called, with beaming countenance, above all the din, "Adolf, tiens!"

Adolf, standing on the next table, caught the globe deftly.

The performers were everywhere, now on the chairs, now on the tables. The clowns cackled; the accordion wailed.

"Fritz, tiens!"

The globes flew back and forth again, over the heads of the clowns. Fritz caught them, and spun quickly around:

"Aimée, tiens!"

He threw them straight at Aimée, and though she jumped up quickly, it was too late; the globe crashed to the floor. Fritz burst out laughing, as he looked down on the broken glass from the table on which he stood.

"That's good luck," he said, and laughed; then stopped suddenly, his eyes riveted on the gas fixture.

Aimée had turned away. She had grown pale as she took her place against the wall. The racket continued, though it was almost midnight. The waiters turned down the gas, but the performance did not cease; in fact, they redoubled the noise in the dim half light. From all sides arose an ear-splitting cackling and shrieking. Fritz was walking on his hands across the table under the chandelier.

He was the last to leave. He was as excited as though he were drunk.

They walked along in little groups, they gradually separated. Their farewells sounded strange in the darkness. "Night," called Mr Fillis – nasal as ever.

"Good night, good night."…

At last, all was quiet, and the Four Devils sauntered along in their accustomed silence. They no longer cared to talk, though Fritz could not settle down; he spun his good hat on the end of his cane.

Finally they reached their lodgings, and bade each other good night.

As soon as he reached the bedroom, Fritz opened both windows wide and began to whistle loudly, so that the sound carried far out into the street.

"Are you crazy?" asked Adolf. "What the devil ails you, anyway?"

Fritz merely laughed: "Il fait si beau temps," was all he answered, and again resumed his whistling.

Downstairs, Aimée also had opened a window. Louise, on the point of undressing, asked her to close it, but the other remained motionless, staring into the dark street.

Until now she had not understood why his eyes stared so vacantly when he looked at her; why he sounded so bored when he spoke to her; and why he seemed half deaf when she said anything to him. They were no longer the same beings: yesterday he had even refused to powder her arms. He had dashed in, rushed and impatient as ever, but when she stretched out her arms, he had merely stared vacantly at them, and, then, collecting his thoughts, roughly burst out:

"Oh, powder them yourself!" and walked away.

Without understanding she had slowly powdered first the

left arm, then the right.

Never had she realised that anyone could suffer so.

Aimée rested her head against the window frame, sudden, scalding tears rolling down her cheeks. Now she knew everything; now she understood.

Suddenly she raised her head: Fritz was beginning to hum loudly to himself. It was the *Love Waltz*. Louder and louder grew his humming; finally he began to sing.

How carefree it sounded, how happy! Every note was a stab, and still she listened: the song seemed to recall her entire life, everything!

How well she remembered it all, from the very first day she had seen him!

Louise called to her again, and she closed the window mechanically. But she did not go to bed. She sat down in a dark corner.

Ah yes, how well she remembered it all.

THREE

How clearly Aimee could visualise Fritz and Adolf, the first time they appeared, when they were to be "adopted" by Father Cecchi.

It was early, Louise and Aimée were still in bed.

The boys had stood in the corner, hanging their heads; they wore linen trousers, though it was midwinter, and Fritz had a straw hat.

Father Cecchi make them strip, and examined them carefully, pinching their legs and tapping their chests until they wept, while the old woman who had brought them stood stiffly by, a shrivelled figure, mumbling to herself. Nothing about her moved, except the black flowers on her hat; these seemed to tremble a bit. She never asked a question, merely kept her eyes fixed on the boys, as they obeyed Cecchi's commands.

Aimée and Louise watched from the bed. Father Cecchi continued to probe and tap.

Finally they were "adopted."

The old woman never said a word. She did not touch the boys, nor say "good-bye" to them. She appeared, all the while her black flowers were quivering, to have been seeking something that she could not find. So she walked out of the door, slowly and uncertainly, closing it behind her.

Fritz gave a long scream, as if he had been stabbed.

Then he and Adolf walked back into the corner and sat down, their chins on their knees, their fists firmly braced against the floor, mute as statues.

Father Cecchi chased them into the kitchen to peel potatoes, sending Aimée and Louise after them. All four sat silently around the bowl.

"Where do you come from?" Louise asked. The boys did not answer. With tightly closed lips, they stared at the floor.

After a while, Aimée whispered: "Was that your mother?"

Still they did not answer, but sat with heaving breasts, sobbing to themselves. All that one heard was the splash of the potatoes as they dropped into the water.

"Is she dead?" Louise whispered in her turn. The boys still made no answer, and the little girls kept looking from one to the other, until they began to cry softly, first Aimée and then Louise.

The next day, the boys began to work. They learned the Chinese Dance and the Peasants' Dance. Three weeks later the four of them appeared in public.

Whenever they were to dance, they stood in the wings, Aimée with Fritz, Louise with Adolf. Their eyes were fixed in a glassy stare; their tongues tried to moisten their lips which were parched with fear, as they listened to the music of the orchestra.

"Pull your coat down," said Aimée, scarcely able to control her own feverish excitement, as she straightened Fritz's jacket, which had slipped.

"Commence!" cried Cecchi from the first wings. The curtain went up; it was time to go on. They did not see the footlights; they did not see the people. With a terrifying smile, they performed the steps in which they had been drilled, moving their lips as they counted the beats, their eyes riveted on Cecchi who was beating time with his foot.

"To the left," Aimée whispered to Fritz, who was never quite sure of himself. She broke out in a cold perspiration – it was such an effort to remember for both of them.

The four children looked like little wax figures turning on a music box.

The audience applauded and gave them a curtain call. Oranges were thrown on to the stage. The children picked up the fruit, smiling gratefully, though they knew it must be handed over to Father Cecchi, who ate the oranges, when he drank brandy and water in the evenings, and played cards with the agent, Watson.

Sometimes the two played all night in Cecchi's lodgings. Whenever they quarrelled, the children would awaken, looking at them wide-eyed until they fell back into the deep slumber of exhaustion.

Time passed.

Cecchi's troupe joined a circus, and all four of them went through the mill. Rehearsals began at eight-thirty. With chattering teeth, they dressed, and began work in the dusk of the tent. Louise and Aimée walk the tight-rope, balancing with two flags, and Father Cecchi, leaning against the railing, gave directions.

Then the horse was brought in, and Fritz was to execute the jockey-leap. Father Cecchi, with a long whip, shouted the commands. Fritz leaped and leaped – but in vain. He fell at the gate, and as he leaned dizzily against the horse, the whip whistled through the air, raising long welts on the boy's legs.

Father Cecchi continued his commands. Fighting down his sobs, Fritz leaped again, and again. But he always missed and fell.

Old wounds on his body opened and bled so that his tights were spotted with blood.

And Father Cecchi kept crying, "Encore, encore!" Breathless, sobbing, the boy leaped, his face contorted with pain. The whip struck him, and in despair he screamed, "I can't!" But he had to try again.

The horse was beaten more than ever, and flew on with the sobbing child, whose limbs quivered with pain. "I can't, oh, I can't."

All the performers watched mutely from the boxes.

"Encore!" cried Cecchi. Fritz leaped again. Pale, with white lips, Aimée sat hidden, watching with horror and indignation. But Cecchi would not stop. It lasted over an hour, – an hour and a quarter. Fritz's body was one bleeding wound. He fell, and fell again, stamping his feet on the sand with anguish.

No, it could not be done. He was finally dismissed with a curse.

Aimée ran from the box; moaning with sympathy, she hid Fritz behind some barrel-staves. Breathless, with clenched hands, he sputtered curses – vulgar street words, phrases of the stable.

Aimée sat quite still. Only her white lips quivered.

For a long time they lay hidden back of that pile of staves. Fritz's head had dropped against the wall; he had fallen into the sleep of painful exhaustion, while Aimée, pale as a little spectre, sat watching over his sleep.

FOUR

Years passed by. The four had at last grown up.

Father Cecchi was dead. He had been kicked to death by a horse.

But the four stuck together, through all the ups and downs that they encountered, sometimes working with large shows, sometimes with small.

How clearly Aimée could visualise the bare, whitewashed structure in that provincial town where they had worked one winter! How cold it was! Three braziers were brought in before the performance, filling the whole building with smoke, so that breathing became difficult. Out in the stalls stood the artists, blue with the cold, holding their bare arms over a brazier, while the clowns leaped about the icy floor, in their cloth shoes, just to keep their feet warm.

The Cecchi troupe worked at various things. They danced, Fritz as Aimée's partner. Aimée was also première equestrienne, and Fritz, dressed as groom, tightened her saddle girth. The troupe worked hard, filling out a good half of the programme.

But the show was a failure nonetheless. Every week another horse disappeared from the stalls, sold to buy fodder for the others. The performers who had money went away; those who were forced to remain went hungry, until the inevitable happened, and they were forced to close.

Horses, costumes, everything was taken from them. Representatives of the law had stepped in, and made a clean sweep.

The few performers who remained sat silent and disconsolate in the dark room. They couldn't leave. They did not even know where to go.

In the stable, on a feed box, the director sat in front of the empty stalls and wept, continuously mumbling a string of curses in any language that happened to occur to him.

Otherwise not a sound: the place was dead. Only the dogs, overlooked by the authorities, lay sadly on a pile of straw, with anxious, troubled eyes.

The Cecchi troupe entered the deserted restaurant. The proprietor had locked the buffet, and taken away the glasses. Tables and chairs, thick with dust, stood about in disorder.

The four sat down gloomily in the corner. They had just returned from their daily walk to the post-office. There were letters from various agents, but they contained only refusals.

Fritz opened and read them. The other three sat near, not daring to put a question. He opened one letter after another, slowly, apprehensively, read it, and laid it aside. The others watched in troubled silence.

Then he said: "Nothing."

And once more they sat in front of those fateful letters that brought nothing.

Finally Fritz burst out: "We cannot go on this way. We must try for a specialty." Adolf shrugged his shoulders. "Every line is overcrowded already," he said, adding sarcastically, "invent something new, why don't you?"

"Trapeze work always means good pay," remarked Fritz in a suppressed voice.

The others made no reply, and Fritz said as before: "We could work in the cupolas."

Silence again. Then Adolf cried, almost angrily, "Are you so perfectly sure of your limbs?" Fritz did not answer, and gloomy silence fell once more.

"We might separate, you know," suggested Adolf hoarsely.

The same idea had occurred to them all, but each tried to avoid suggesting it. Now it was out, and Adolf added, gazing into the gloom of the deserted place, "One cannot be everlastingly starving at the same thing!"

He spoke in a suppressed, excited voice, like one who is debating the impossible; but Fritz continued silent and motionless, staring at the floor.

They rose and filed out mutely, through those long halls. How cold and dark they were!

Softly, in an almost inaudible voice, Aimée said to Fritz, who was walking beside her, "Fritz, I will work in the air with you."

Fritz stopped: "I knew it," he said softly, and squeezed her hand.

Louise and Adolf said nothing.

They decided to remain in the city. Fritz pawned their rings, as a last resort, and Adolf continued to communicate with the agents.

But Fritz and Aimée worked. They had put up their trapeze in the "Pantheon" and began to work regularly, every day. They adapted some floor exercises to the trapeze and tortured their sweating, aching bodies for hours on end. From time to time Fritz's commands could be heard; then they were forced to rest, sitting side-by-side on the same board with tired, exhausted smiles.

As they grew accustomed to the work, they began the Hanlon-

FOUR

Volta exercises, attempting leaps from one swing to another, only to fall into the outstretched net. But they persevered, encouraging each other with cries of "En avant! Ça va! Encore!"

Fritz at last was able to make his distance. Aimée fell. But they kept on. Their very souls looked from their eyes, their muscles responded like steel springs, their voices rang like subdued battle cries. At last they both succeeded. One followed the other with wrapped, feverish interest: "En avant! Du courage!"

Aimée had got across; her muscles quivered as she hung from the farthest trapeze. She tried again, and succeeded. A great joy overwhelmed her. Both of them became intoxicated by the strength of their bodies. They flew past each other; rested again, dripping with perspiration, but smiling happily, hand in hand. Overcome by their joy, they praised each other's bodies, stroked the muscles that had served them so well, and looked at one another shining eyes.

"Ça va, ça va," they shouted, and laughed aloud. Then they began to try more difficult feats; they thought up new combinations. Planning and calculating, with the zeal of inventors they plunged into their practice, made plans, and tried all sorts of experiments. Fritz scarcely slept: thoughts of his work kept him awake at night.

In the morning, before sunrise, he was knocking at Aimée's door, to awaken her. Standing outside, while waiting for her to dress, he would elaborate his plans, explaining in a loud voice, while she, with equal eagerness, called back replies, their happy voices filling the house.

Louise sat up in bed rubbing her eyes. She had begun to attend their rehearsals, and became quite carried away by the progress made by Aimée and Fritz. She called to them and applauded. Then they would reply from above, and the hall rang with their happy voices.

Only Adolf sat mutely in a corner near the stable. One day, he too strolled in to watch, but no one said a word to him.

FIVE

Practice over, their strength gave out, and they fell heavily into the net below; Fritz leaped to the ground and carefully lifted Aimée down, holding her in his outstretched arms like a child.

They changed their clothes and went into a little tavern across the way for dinner. They began to speak of the future: when they might get engagements, what salary they could demand, what name they should assume. They knew that success awaited them now.

The two silent ones became loquacious. They laughed, as they built up their future, and Fritz kept inventing new tricks, always new ones.

"If only we dared," said Fritz, his voice hoarse with eagerness, "if we only dared!"

And Aimée replied, looking straight at him, "Why not? If you are willing."

Something in her voice touched Fritz: "You are brave," he said, suddenly, and looked into those trusting eyes, shining into his. Whereupon they sat, with heads against the wall, gazing into space, weaving daydreams.

One day, they tried that last leap, the trick they had decided would be their great feature. They succeeded. Flying backwards, they reached the trapeze.

From below, they heard a shout. It was Adolf. With upturned face, and beaming eyes, he was crying, "Bravo, bravo," so that the empty hall re-echoed. "Bravo," he cried once more, overcome with admiration.

And they began to discuss it, all four of them, from above and below, explaining and questioning.

On this day, they ate together, and on the next as well. They all talked about the tricks, as though all of them were taking part. Fritz explained: "Oui, mes enfants, if only the four of us worked together. You two above with rigid bars, and we two below, with our death leap. Oh, if we could only do that!"

He began to explain his plan to them, meticulously outlining all details, but Adolf said nothing, and Louise made no reply.

Next day, however, Adolf asked, standing with downcast eyes and shuffling feet, "Are you going to practice this afternoon?"

No, they never rehearsed in the afternoon. "You see," added Adolf, "we are wasting time, our muscles are getting stiff."

That afternoon Adolf and Louise began to practice. The other two came and watched, encouraging, and directing. Fritz sat there happily, playing with Aimée's hand.

"Ça va, ça va," they both shouted from below.

Up above, Louise and Adolf were flying boldly from swing to swing.

Now, they knew, they would stay together.

Rehearsals were over at last, and their act was ready. They worked as Fritz had wished, call themselves The Four Devils, and had costumes designed and made to order in Berlin.

They made their debut in Breslau. Then they travelled from city to city, and always enjoyed immense success.

Aimée had undressed and gone to bed. Sleepless she lay,

staring into the darkness. Yes, how vividly it all came back, from the very first day. They had spent their entire lives together, side by side.

And now *she* had come, the stranger; and at the thought the acrobat girl ground her teeth in sheer, desperate, physical rage – yes, *she* had come to destroy him!

What did she want of him, with her cat's eyes? What did she want with her provoking smile? What did she want, why did she offer herself to him like a common drab? To ruin him utterly, to snatch him from her, to destroy his strength: annihilate him.

Aimée bit into her sheet, wadded up her pillow, but could find no rest for her feverish hands. Her mind could not summon up enough angry rebukes or coarse accusations; she wept again, overcome by all that paralysing misery that pursued her night and day.

SIX

Fritz lay with closed eyes, his head resting on the lap of his beloved.

More and more slowly her pointed nails glided over his fair hair.

Fritz lay with closed eyes, his head resting lightly on her lap. So this was real: he, Fritz Schmidt, a Frankfurt street urchin, a fatherless boy, whose mother, one day, more drunk than usual, had jumped into the river, and whose grandmother had sold him and his brother together for twenty marks. So this was real: he, Fritz Schmidt, called Cecchi, of The Four Devils, had become her lover – the lover of The Lady in the Box. It was his neck that rested on her knees; his arm that encircled her body, his throat to which her lips were pressed.

He half opened his eyes, and saw with the same uncomprehending, intoxicated admiration, her delicate hand, so soft, so untouched by work, her arched fingernails, her delicate white skin, that he loved to kiss so long and tenderly.

Yes, it was he, Fritz Cecchi, who sensed the fragrance of her body, so close to him, who felt the texture of her clothing, delicate as clouds. How his hands loved to fondle her!

For him alone, she waited each night beside the high grating, shivering, as if with the cold. She led him into the little garden of the palace, and clung to him behind every clump of bushes. His lips she called her "blossom", his arms, her "despair". How strangely she spoke. It was all so queer!

Fritz Cecchi smiled and closed his eyes again. She saw the smile, bent over him, and passed her lips across his face. Fritz continue to smile, enchanted by this miracle.

"How strange this is," he murmured softly, and continued in the same tone, "how strange this is," turning his head slightly from side to side.

"What?" she asked.

"This," he replied, and again lay still, as if afraid of waking from a dream. But he continued to smile, mentally repeating her name, over and over, surprised at it, for it was one of the great names of Europe, and had reached even him – like a legend.

Slowly he reopened his eyes, and looked at her. Then, laughing like a boy, he seized her two ears, squeezing them harder and harder. Even this was permitted him – even this.

He half rose, resting his head on her shoulder, and with the same smile, gazed about the room. He was lord of all this, all that belonged to her, the thousand fragile curiosities that covered the queer spindle-legged furniture, which at first he had scarcely dared to touch. He, the juggler, had fingered these objects gingerly, as if they would fall to pieces in his hands; but now he could gaily play ball with an art table or balance an entire what-not, while she laughed and laughed.

The paintings were strange to him – pictures of ancestors in the costume of the Restoration Period, with dress swords and gauntlets. There were moments when he laughed loudly at these portraits, like a street gamin, because he, Fritz Schmidt, was sitting here with her, the scion of such ancestors, and that she was now his very own.

Finally she asked, "What are you laughing at?"

"Oh, yes," he replied, and suddenly stopped, "how strange this is, how strange this is…"

He experienced a peculiar, half-happy, half-timid astonishment that he should be here – actually the master here.

For so he felt himself. Was she not his? In his unconscious brain still dwelt the thought of male possessing female; he, the active one, who in his consuming passion was still the dominant force.

But all these primitive conceptions disappeared, although Fritz had always prided himself on subduing and taming them. He became powerless and helpless in his silent renewed admiration of her, whose most insignificant words had a different sound and inflection; whose body was of such strange exotic perfection, so undeveloped and so delicate.

He grew tractable and timid; and suddenly opened his eyes to make sure that it was no dream, stroking her dainty, slender fingers. Yes, it was all true!

Her hands passed more and more uncertainly through his hair, while he lay, as if asleep.

"But what do you want of me?" he asked.

"You stupid man," she whispered, and put her mouth close to his cheek, "You stupid man." She continued to whisper; the sound of her voice excited him even more than her embraces, "You stupid man, you stupid man!"

Then he sat up, and pressing her head against his breast, looked at her with indescribable tenderness. "Could you sleep here?" he asked, and rocked in his arms like a child, until their eyes met, and both of them laughed.

"You stupid man."

His eyes kindled; he seized her; and swiftly, without a word,

SIX

carried her in his outstretched arms into the room beyond. There a pale blue lamp glowed like a sleepy eye.

Day broke as they parted. But in all corners, on the treads of the stairs, in the garden around the quiet house that looked so aristocratic and so honourable, they drew out the hours of their rendezvous, while she still whispered like a refrain, "You stupid man!"

At last Fritz tore himself away, and the iron door closed after him. But, seeing her standing still, he returned and once more took her in his arms. Suddenly he laughed aloud as he stood beside her in front of that great palace. As if their thoughts had met, she also laughed and she looked up at the home of her fathers.

And he began, feeling a delightful sense of triumph under his curiosity, to ask questions about each of the great stone escutcheons over the windows and the inscriptions on the gateposts. She answered him, still laughing.

The proudest names of all the land were there. He did not know them, but she told something about each one. It was a tale of battles, honours, victories. He laughed.

Here were shields which had defended the throne, escutcheons as old as the throne of St. Peter.

He laughed.

Inflamed by her own unworthiness, she grew more passionate in her endearments, coarse, almost blasphemous in this dawning light, while she continued her narrative, as if she wished in the telling to tear down the coats-of-arms, and trample them in the mire of her love.

"And that one?" he asked. "And that?"

She went on telling him all about them. It was a tale of centuries. Here thrones had been established, there kingdoms had fallen. This man had been the friend of an emperor; that caused the death of a king. She went on and on, whispering with a teasing sort of scorn, while she leaned against the shoulder of the acrobat, and gave herself up entirely to this sensation of defilement.

He, too, became intoxicated by it.

It seemed as if both of them beheld this annihilation, and were enjoying it – enjoying from minute to minute, the fall of this great House, with its portals, escutcheons, shields, memorial tablets, and turrets, the collapse of this great House that was being ground beneath the wheels of their passion.

Finally she tore herself away and ran up the path. At the little door, she turned once again, and as a last joke, threw a mocking kiss at the coat-of-arms on the pediment.

Fritz went home, feeling as if he had wings on his feet. At the same time, he was intensely aware of all her endearments.

All around him, the great city was coming to life. Carts rumbled along the streets, laden with all the treasures of the flower market: violets, early roses, cowslips, forsythia.

Fritz began to sing. Under his breath, he hummed the words of the *Love Waltz*:

>*Amour, amour,*
>*Oh, bel oiseau,*
>*Chante, chante,*
>*Chante toujours.*

The carts clattered past him – the entire street was alive with fragrance. The flower vendors who sat on the drivers' seats wrapped in great blankets, turned round and smiled at him.

He never stopped singing, until he reached the street where he lived. It was silent and still half dark, the houses stood so close and high. Fritz now walked more slowly. Still humming, he scanned the house, from top to bottom, before entering.

He gave a sudden start. Had he seen a face peering through the glass of an upper window?

Pale, with bated breath, Aimée listened at the door. Yes, that was he:

> *Amour, amour,*
> *Oh, bel oiseau,*
> *Chante, chante,*
> *Chante toujours.*

He locked his door and all was still.

As pale as a sleep-walker, her hands pressed against her heart, Aimée crept into bed. Motionless she lay, staring out into the grey light of the dawn.

SEVEN

It was late when Fritz Cecchi awoke and, on account of his exhaustion, consciousness returned very gradually, as he lay watching Adolf rubbing himself down with a wet towel.

"Are you really awake?" asked Adolf, sarcastically.

"Yes," was all Fritz answered, as he continued to watch his brother.

"It's high time you got up," added Adolf in the same tone.

"Yes," said Fritz, but continued, without moving, to stare at the strong, undefiled body of his brother, observing the lively play of the muscles.

Suddenly a blind anger, the bitter, miserable wrath of the vanquished, overcame him. He raised his arms, and felt their weakness, braced his feet against the foot-board, and realised the softness of the leg muscles. Straightway he was overwhelmed by a wild primitive resentment against himself, his body, his sex; above all against her, the thief, the robber, the Delilah!

His fury was unreasoning. All he knew was that he longed to beat her to death, like a madman, with clenched fists; beat her to pieces while she shrieked and laughed; until she couldn't move, and then trample on her with both feet.

SEVEN

Again he raised his arms, clasping his hands, and again felt the impotence of the weakened muscles, as he gritted his teeth with rage.

Adolf walked out, banging the door behind him.

Then Fritz leaped from the bed, and began to examine his body. He attempted a number of exercises and failed. He tried floor gymnastics with no greater success. His weary limbs shook stubbornly. Again he tried, striking himself, pinching his flesh with his fingernails. In vain. He could do nothing. He beat his head against the wall, and tried again, only to fail.

Exhausted, he sat down before the great mirror, and went over every muscle of his inert and unstrung body.

Then it was true: they robbed one of everything, health, strength, muscular power! It was true! He would soon lose everything: work, position, reputation. Yes, it was true.

He would go the same road as the others, soon it would be all over with him. It would be with him as it was with *The Stars*, who had dragged two women from city to city, and beat them, until they had to be shut up in an insane asylum.

He would end like the juggler, Charles, who had lived with the singer Adelina; his limbs had grown soft as a drunkard's, and finally he had hanged himself.

Or Hubert, who had eloped with an inn-keeper's wife, and now rode at county fairs; or the juggler, Paul, who had fallen for Anita, the knife-thrower, and was now barker for a tent show.

Yes, they made a wreck of one's body.

But he would not surrender. Frantically, he began again to torture his muscles in an effort to harness his strength; to spur on every fibre of his body. This time he succeeded.

Wildly, he slapped on his clothes, and scarcely buttoning them, dashed out. He must practice, practice in the circus, on the trapeze.

EIGHT

Adolf, Aimée, and Louise were already at work; he saw them hanging from the bars in their grey work-smocks.

Fritz changed his clothes and began some ground-work. He walked on his hands, balancing first on the right, then on the left, until all his body quivered.

The others watched silently from their swings.

Then, suddenly and eagerly, he swung himself up into the net opposite Aimée. Hanging by his arms, he took long swings, stretching his slender body into a straight line, and began.

Aimée sat motionless. With her heavy, sleepless eyes she stared steadily at this being that she loved, this man whom she adored, who had just come from a love night with another woman.

Had they not lived side by side for years? Had their bodies not touched every day? She measured him with her eyes: his neck that had carried her, his arms that had caught her, his thighs that she had clasped. The routine of their calling, all the knowledge of their work, increased her misery.

New, overwhelmed by frightful suffering – actual physical suffering, that only she could feel – she stared at Fritz as he worked opposite her.

But it was Fritz himself who aroused her last.

"Why don't you begin?" he asked harshly.

"Oh, yes."

She gave a start and mechanically rose in the swing. For an instant their eyes met, and in that fleeting second, seeing her pale face, staring eyes, and rigid, motionless body, Fritz realised everything.

At the same moment he was seized by an unconquerable disgust at the thought of coming in contact with the body of a woman – a feeling of revolt against touching any other than her whom he loved. There welled up within him an insurmountable, chilling repugnance amounting almost to hatred.

"Begin!" cried Adolf.

"Do begin," called Louise.

Still they hesitated. Then they flew past each other in the air. Deathly pale, they turned and flew again. He caught her, but she fell. They tried again, but he fell.

They began all over again, eye to eye, seeming to grow paler every moment. Both fell, Fritz first.

Louise and Adolf laughed aloud up on their swings.

"Well, this surely is your lucky day," Adolf called.

"Someone has given him the evil eye," Louise cried. And again they laughed together.

The other two continued their practice and failed again, Aimée let go, and Fritz scolded loudly down in the net. Finally they were all scolding, excited and angry, calling in loud shrill voices – all but Aimée. She sat still with staring eyes, pale as death.

Fritz climbed back and they resumed work. Simultaneously the same rage flared up in both. Screaming they clutched each other, embracing wildly. It was no longer practice – it was a struggle. They no longer met, grasped, embraced; they wrestled rather, and seized one another like animals. Their bodies seemed aglow as they tested their strength in desperate battle. They did not stop. They no longer gave commands. Senselessly, blinded by brutal unconquerable hatred, they fought a desperate duel in the air.

Suddenly Aimée dropped with a scream. For a moment she lay motionless in the net. Fritz mounted to his swing, and with clenched teeth, his face set as a mask, regarded the woman he had vanquished.

He rose on the trapeze, announcing: "She cannot work anymore. Let her take the upper swing; Louise can work here with me."

He spoke harshly, as though he had the right to command. No one replied, but slowly Louise began to glide from the dome to Aimée's swing. Aimée spoke not a word. Like a broken animal, she half raised herself in the net, and then climbed slowly up to the swing in the dome.

Work was resumed. But Fritz's strength was gone. His very bitterness reacted on him. His arms gave out; he fell, Louise falling upon him.

"What in the world is the matter with you?" cried Adolf. "Are you sick? You take the top; perhaps you can manage that. This will never do."

Fritz made no reply. He sat with bowed head, like one who has received a blow. Then he said, mumbling through clenched teeth, "Yes, we had better trade places – for today."

He climbed out of the net and walked away, the knuckles on his clenched hands glistening white. He thought he heard the attendants whispering his name, and sneaked past them, filled with shame, like a whipped dog.

In the dressing-room he dropped to the mattress. All sensation had left his body. He was conscious only of his eyes. How they smarted and burned! But there was no rest for him. He began to practice again. As one tortures an aching tooth, or presses one's finger on a boil, so he continued to test his weary limbs. He tried feverishly to execute this or that trick; but he could do nothing. Again he threw himself on the mattress, only to leap up and try again. These repeated struggles exhausted him completely, yet he refused to give up.

So the day passed. He never left the circus, but haunted the ring, like a bad conscience hovering about the scene of a crime.

In the evening he worked in the dome with Louise. He struggled like a maniac to make his stubborn limbs respond; desperately, he forced his quivering muscles to obey.

He succeeded: once, twice, again. He flew over, and flew back, then rested.

He saw nothing. Not the dome, nor the boxes, nor Adolf; only that distant trapeze, and Louise swinging in front of him. It seemed to him as though the pounding blood were going to burst his brain. Then he leaped, grasped for Louise's leg, and with a scream fell into the billowing net below.

There was not a sound in the whole huge building. All was silent, thinking he was dead.

Then Fritz lifted his shoulders. Where was he? With a tremendous effort, he recalled it all, – the arena, the net, the black frame-work of spectators, the boxes, and *her*. Overcome by despair, more through his humiliation than from the pain of the fall, he lifted his clenched fists and collapsed.

The three others had stopped their performance, and were calling confusedly to each other. Adolf had at once dropped down a rope. He and two assistants lifted Fritz from the net,

EIGHT

supporting him; so that he appeared to walk.

Finally Aimée slid slowly down the rope. She walked like a blind person, seeing nothing.

Two performers were standing at the entrance. "That net surely saved his life," said one.

"Yes, indeed," replied the other, "except for that, he would be cold and stiff by now."

Aimée gave a sudden start; she had heard the words, and as if she was seeing them for the first time, she measured with a single lingering glance the net, the ropes, and the swings – those fearfully high swings. One of the artists read her glance aright.

"They are damnably high," he said.

Aimée merely nodded, quite deliberately.

All was quiet again, and the performance continued.

In the dressing-room, Fritz had risen from the mattress and was standing before his mirror. He had not been injured, only stunned by the fall.

Adolf was busy dressing, and both were silent. Finally Adolf burst out: "You see for yourself, this can't go on."

Fritz did not answer, but averted his gaze from the pale face looking at him in the mirror. Just as Adolf was ready, they heard Louise rapping at the door.

"Won't you ever be ready?" demanded Adolf. "They are waiting for us."

Fritz took down his watch from the corner of the mirror, and went out to join the sisters, who were waiting in silence. They walked home in silence, too, Fritz beside Louise. The humiliation seared his very soul, as though it were a physical wound in his breast.

NINE

Fritz and Adolf had been in bed a long time, and Adolf was sleeping heavily with his mouth open, as acrobats usually do when their bodies lie relaxed in slumber. But Fritz could get no rest; he lay on his back, sleepless, in dull despair.

So it had happened, at last, and so soon! He was no longer fit for work. This one thought went round and round in his mind: no longer fit for work. Slowly, and with infinite weariness, he made it clear to himself, how it had all come about, day after day, night after night. Quietly and wearily, he visualised everything: the blue room, the high bed, himself and her; the yellow room with the lounge behind the screen, and the portraits on the wall, himself and her; the staircase where the lamp went out, himself and her; and the garden, in which he kept turning back.

And now it was all over. He was reaping what he had sown. Ah, he knew it well. Thus his thoughts kept drifting lazily, stupidly along. But even as he had been ruined so he would ruin her. Yes, he would do that. Some night he would go there and unlock the door. Then when he was there with her (and his thoughts must pause to linger on the blue room, with himself and her), he would ring wildly to arouse the whole house, so that her husband and the servants and the maids should come and see her – *her*!

Yes, he could do this; he would! And suddenly, seeing it all before his eyes, he said: "That's what I'll do, and do it now!"

All repose left him. Why not do it now that the plan was fresh, his anger hot, his resolution strong? He would go immediately.

Rapidly, without turning on the lights, he collected his clothes and dressed very quietly, in order not to awaken Adolf, while constantly before his eyes hovered the vision of himself and her in the middle of the blue room. There he would have his revenge.

In his haste, he knocked against the chair, and immediately sat down on the bed, overcome by fear lest Adolf might awake.

Then he went on dressing, with bated breath. He must go now!

A careless step disturbed Adolf, who, turning in bed, mumbled drowsily, "What the devil ails you?" and then added, "Where are you going?" Fritz did not answer. Half-dressed as he was, he crept under the bed clothes to hide, and found himself trembling like a trapped thief.

But soon after, hearing Adolf's regular breathing, he began again, dressing as he lay in bed, shivering with apprehension, as if he was stealing his own clothes.

Ready at last! He felt his way to the door, going carefully along the wall, crafty as a drunkard who is trying to creep towards his bottle without being seen.

And he succeeded in opening the door, closing it and sneaking down the stairs and out of the house. He felt that he had no more shame than a dog. He even said to himself, "Tomorrow I shan't be able to work, either." But with the logic of despair, he murmured, "I might as well go to the devil altogether."

He began to run faster and faster past the houses, keeping

carefully in the shadows.

At home no one had heard him, except Aimée. She had gotten up and followed him, gliding down the stairs, out of the house, and along the other side of the street. Like one shadow pursuing another, she followed him through the silent streets.

Fritz reached the palace with the iron fence. He entered. His footsteps died away. Aimée stood hidden in a doorway opposite the palace window. She saw a light moving on the first floor, two shadows slipping past lace curtains. There they were. The light reappeared, she saw the shadows again, upstairs. Then the light went out, and only a bluish glow glimmered in the last window.

With bated breath, in the throes of consuming jealousy, she stared at those windows, while one picture after another came to torture her as she waited. All those mental visions that comprise the ultimate misery of the deserted, appeared before this acrobat girl, chaste though she still was. They seemed to be vividly depicted on that windowpane, behind which he was, behind which they were, together. And her whole life that had been spent in self-sacrifice, her whole existence, filled with uncomplaining surrender, all her dearest hopes, all her tenderest thoughts, every dream for a life together banished at once. Her whole life, bit by bit, memory after memory, thought upon thought, was shattered, engulfed, completely wiped out. Nothing was left her: no surrender, no tenderness, no willingness to sacrifice – nothing. How humiliated she felt, how alone; everything fell back into its elemental beginnings. There remained nearly the all-powerful, all-destroying impulse.

Hours passed. Aimée felt she could suffer no more. Like a somnambulist she stared dully at the pale blue glow. Then the garden gate opened, and shut again. There he was! And Aimée in her agony, saw him walk slowly past her, a grey figure, in the grey light of the dawning day.

TEN

"Aimée," said Louise, as if she were trying to wake her sister, "are you asleep?" Aimée raised her arm automatically and bound up her long hair. "One would really think so," pursued Louise. Aimée was sitting in front of her mirror, in which she surveyed her reflection, without moving, as if two sleepers were staring at one another with open eyes.

Slowly she put on her blouse, got up, and went out with the same strange manner; it seemed as though she were following an apparition, she walked like an automaton, as if her soul had fallen asleep and her body were dead. Louise followed, and both went out into the dark place where Fritz was waiting on a swing. Aimée had never worked so well as she did today; in a mechanical rhythm she caught herself, let go, and flew. She was working with Fritz again, and her calmness seemed to react upon him. Like the lifeless cogs of a machine, they came together, separated, and came together again. Then they rested on opposite swings.

In all that great hall, Aimée's eyes were fixed on one thing, alone: his body. This agile body, this heaving breast, the gasping mouth, the hotly pulsating veins could all go still and cold. His spring-like muscles, the hands that caught her, his neck, now

TEN

so full of life, would all grow still and cold. His arms would be motionless, his muscles like a stone, his forehead cold, his neck stiff and dead, his breast so high and still. Then his hand would drop, oh, so heavily if one were to lift it. Arms, legs, and hands – dead!

They worked again. They flew and then met. Every touch spurred her on: however warm he might be now, he should grow cold; however much he quivered now, he should suddenly become quite still. She no longer dwelt upon the reason, thought no more of herself. She saw always the vision of Fritz dead, – cold and lifeless. That was all.

And like one mentally deranged who keeps following his secret mania, she became sly and deceptive. Like an opium fiend, who lives only to satisfy his craving, she became wonderfully inventive. She developed the callousness of the monomaniac. She pursued Fritz whom she had so long shyly avoided. When the rehearsal was over, she commenced to work alone. She adapted all the exercises of the lower swings to the ones in the cupola. She called down to Fritz, detaining him in the ring, while she asked questions and solicited advice, flattering him as an apprentice does his master. She dared everything up there in the dome. She played with death, shamelessly enticing him, she kept watching his uncertainty, as if to gauge its extent. She sought help from the weakness that he tried so hard to hide. She attempted the most daring feats, crying: "We'll show them what we can do! We won't let them get ahead of us!"

So she lured him on. He gave advice, and finally climbed up the swing rope to join her on the trapeze. Meanwhile she flew past him among the rattling swings. From trapeze to trapeze she flew over the yawning abyss. And he, driven by an irresistible impulse, began to follow her lead, while she spurred him on with her shouts. She had the strength of fever in her taut body, and he called upon his last ounce of endurance, as in a struggle for life and death.

She cried, "Ça va, ça va," and he swung into position and caught hold: "Ça va, ça va!"

The artists who were going in and out of the arena stood still to watch them. He grew ever more enthusiastic, daring all that she dared, as she led the way from swing to swing with wildly fluttering hair. They met and seized each other. How cold her body was!

Finally she stopped. But he continued practicing. She sat hunched on her swing, encouraging him with muffled growling comments. She sat in the dark and watched him. Fritz moaned, and in dropping seized the swinging rope, so that in the darkness, it looked as if he were falling all the way. Aimée remained on her swing. She heard him fall into the net, then walk out, over the soft sand of the ring.

It was dark. Only from the dome filtered down a subdued light. The whole tremendous building was wrapped in silence. Aimée continued to cower between the net and the rope; then she got up, making the hasps that held the swings and ropes rattle softly. She lifted and examined them; then, like a shadow, busied herself about something there in the dark. The brass knobs gleamed like cat's eyes, otherwise, all was dark. Softly the ropes rubbed against each other; that was the only sound.

Aimée busied herself for a long time up there in the dome. Then a loud voice sounded from below in the ring. It was Fritz, calling, "Aimée, Aimée!"

"I'm coming," she replied. Aimée seized the right hand rope, and slowly glided down hovering silently, for a moment, over the man waiting below. Then she repeated, "I'm coming," and a

TEN

moment later stood at his side.

ELEVEN

The Four Devils were to have a benefit. It was the evening before, just after the performance; the audience was filing out of the circus. Adolf knocked on Aimée's and Louise's door, and all four of them walked along the hall. Not a word was spoken, and they quietly took their usual table in the restaurant. Their beer seidels[1] were brought, and they drank in silence. Aimée's every motion, even the slightest like picking up her glass, seemed strangely deliberate and so slow it was as if she were doing everything to a dreary, measured tempo.

There was much noise in the restaurant. Bib and Bob were celebrating their birthday, and a circle of artists sat about the table. One of them was doing sleight-of-hand tricks, the clown Trip was imitating a certain Rigolo by coarsely swinging his hips from side to side. Only The Devils sat quietly in the corner. One by one, the ballet girls disappeared from their places along the wall, their anxious expectation relieved by the arrival of certain hurried gentlemen. At a side table some of the agents were playing cards.

The clowns continued their racket. One of them played an

---

[1] A 'seidel' is a beer mug or glass.

accordion, and half a dozen cri-cris[2] replied. The clown Tom presented his colleague with a cabbage-head filled with snuff, and everyone began to sniffle and sneeze, in chorus. On a table, Trip was still imitating the evolutions of Rigolo.

But the Devils kept quiet.

The billposter came in with his jar and handbag, and began to paste up the next day's announcements on both bulletin boards. The name *Les Quatres Diables* appeared in three places.

Adolf got up and strolled over to inspect the program. He asked one of the agents to translate it, and the latter rose from the card table and slowly translated, while Adolf listened attentively.

"Assuring our honoured audience and all our patrons that for this performance we shall offer everything in our power, we subscribe ourselves, respectfully,

Les Quatre Diables."

Adolf nodded as he followed the strange text word for word. Then he returned to his table, still staring at the placard with its peculiar lettering, finally remarking with a satisfied look: "Pretty lettering."

Louise and Fritz got up, too, and walked over to inspect it.

The cri-cris shrieked, enough to burst one's ear-drums. The clown Tom evoked music from little reed instruments which he inserted in his nostrils.

Even Aimée had risen. She stood behind Fritz and Louise, while the agent proceeded to translate the words over again:

---

[2] A musical instrument, somewhat like a rattle.

"We subscribe ourselves respectfully,

Les Quatre Diables."

The cri-cris shrieked. Up on top of the table Trip continued his ridiculous gymnastics.

Then Aimée who was the last to join in, laughed loud and long, while the din gradually subsided, and the Devils went back to their places. Adolf took out the money, and pushed it over beside the seidels.[2] The three others rose, but Fritz announced his intention of staying a little longer. He was not ready to go home.

"Good night," said Adolf and Louise.

"Good night," replied Fritz without moving. Aimée stood still. For a moment, she watched him appraisingly, as if she were haunted by the remembrance of the night before.

"A demain, Aimée," he said airily.

Slowly she turned her eyes aside and murmured, "Good night."

She went out into the great hall, where it was dark. The sign poster had left his lantern on the floor, and in its glow the yellow paper of the billboard stood out. The two others were waiting in the doorway, but she followed them alone, past the tall silent houses. The windows looked down at her from massive stone façades with unfamiliar eyes. How clear the sky was! Aimée looked at the stars: she had been told they were worlds, other worlds, perhaps like ours.

Her gaze returned to the houses, doors, windows, lanterns, and paving stones; how strange they looked; she seemed to be seeing them for the first time.

"Aimée," called Louise.

"Yes, I'm coming." And again she stared at the rows of houses, dark and closed, between which their steps died away. Back of her, she faintly heard the cri-cris, the laughter of the clowns.

"Aimée," called Louise once more.

"Yes." Aimée overtook the others again. The two were standing arm in arm in the light of the streetlamp, waiting for her. Louise threw back her head with an impatient little sigh.

"Good heavens," she exclaimed, "aren't you coming at all?" And leaning on Adolf's arm, under the glow of the lantern, she looked down the dead and unfamiliar street, through which they had just come, and remarked: "I like a street like this." Then with a laugh, she began to repeat those highly amusing words: "We subscribe ourselves respectfully," adding as an afterthought, as she looked down the dark street, "I wonder what it's called?"

"Oh," replied Adolf, "one passes so many little streets." And they went on, past the next row of houses.

TWELVE

Fritz had remained behind. The others at the clown table had invited him to have a glass of beer, but he shook his head. One of the clowns called out, "He has something better. Good-night!" And all of them burst out laughing. By this time, Bib and Bob had constructed a fishing rod, and were angling all the artists' hats down from the clothes racks.

Fritz got up and strolled over to the door that opened directly on the street. He sat down at a table on the terrace under some laurel trees. An intense feeling of boredom and indescribable disgust overwhelmed him. He watched the whispering couples who were walking up and down, affectionately close to each other. In the dark, they occasionally kissed, and laughed lovingly. The women pirouetted, and the men strutted and showed off like beasts of the field in the mating season.

Suddenly Fritz gave a sharp, harsh laugh.

He thought of the clown Tim, whom they called The Gentleman with the Dogs. Yes, Tim was right. He visualised him with his quiet, motionless, melancholy features, like a statue's delicate, red, curved and pathetic mouth – a woman's mouth, it was.

Fritz recalled him at home in his lodgings, in his big room, where he had constructed an entire house for his dogs, a two-

TWELVE

story house in which all the dogs lived. There lay the animals, each in his own little cubicle, their heads thrust through the openings, staring into space with eyes as pathetic as those of the clown himself. And he had sat in their midst. What a quiet company it was! All these dogs had been castrated, – and Tim thought them more human than people. Yes, he was right: people are animals, and the moments in which we really *live* are bestial.

They are animals, that want to be satisfied; they are fools, all of them.

We take care of ourselves, working with the most tremendous effort. We give days, years, our youth, our strength, the freshness of our brain, and one day the animal in us rears his head – the fundamental animal that is in us all.

Fritz laughed. Involuntarily he was conscious of his body, of which he had taken such meticulous care all his life, and which he had ruined in the last three months.

One of the artists came out of the door. He waited a moment, then his wife joined him, and they trotted awkwardly down the sidewalk. Fritz looked after them and continued to laugh. How about those who get married? Didn't they sacrifice their bodies, when they mated for life, ate their daily bread, and had children? Like fat drones they swelled up; developed paunches through their regular habits of life. And they raised children to carry on this existence.

Fools, fools!

Fritz stood looking after the strolling couples that grew more and more affectionate, and disappeared into the shadows.

Within, the clowns continued their racket. The cri-cris shrieked, the sound floating over the heads of all, and reaching the people in the street, like a hymn to foolishness.

Fritz got up, and tossing a coin on the table, walked away. In the restaurant the noise increased. They howled, screamed, and laughed. Fritz began to sing. Whistling, screeching, cackling, they all joined in. With clownish grimaces, gestures of the ring, and mouths awry, they began to sing:

> *Amour, amour,*
> *Oh, bel oiseau,*
> *Chante, chante,*
> *Chante toujours.*

Outside on the terrace everyone stood still, the couples picked in at the windows, laughing merrily. Then two or three of them took up the melody of the clowns. Far out into the darkness, floated the air:

> *Amour, amour,*
> *Oh, bel oiseau,*
> *Chante, chante,*
> *Chante toujours.*

From out on the terrace Fritz watched the ridiculous clowns within, and the amorous couples without, all swaying their heads in time to the music. Suddenly the acrobat began to laugh, wildly, insanely, unable to control himself, as he leaned against a lamp post for support.

A policeman walked up to him, and stared surprised at this gentleman in a high hat who was disturbing the peace. But the gentleman continued to laugh hysterically, as he tried to sing:

> *Amour, amour,*
> *Oh, bel oiseau,*
> *Chante, chante,*
> *Chante toujours.*

Then even the policeman began to laugh, without realising why, as the song swelled lustily within.

TWELVE

Fritz turned sharply on his heel and went – to her.

THIRTEEN

The applause resounded, and Louise appeared again.

Then the attendants began to fold up the big net. It sounded like the furling of the mainsail. The music stopped.

"Monsieur Fritz and Mademoiselle Aimée are going to perform their great leap without the net."

Several attendants began to rake the sand of the ring. Now all was ready. Like a guard at salute, the attendants waited, while the strains of *The Love Waltz* was heard again.

Fritz and Aimée entered hand in hand. Bowing their thanks, they stood amid the flowers that had been tossed to them. Then they climbed up the long ropes, followed by thousands of eyes.

For an instant, they rested side by side.

A shudder swept over the crowd, as Fritz let go and flew across.

Never before had they worked more surely. In the breathless hush, their hands grasped the rattling swings squarely and firmly.

Fritz flew over and back. Aimée's eyes were fixed upon him, large and dull, like two lamps about to go out.

The waltz swelled louder; the play of the swings more violent.

As from a single, suffocating breast, came an apprehensive

murmur of applause.

Aimée unbound her hair, as if she wished to wrap herself in a dark cloak. Standing upright, she waited in the swing for Fritz.

Their great leaps now began. The flew, they rushed across. Their words sounded like bird cries above the music, and thousands watched in troubled bewilderment.

"Aimée, du courage!"

He flew.

"Enfin du courage!"

He seized the bar again.

Aimée saw only him, his body fairly seemed to glow. The applause resounded once more, while the waltz swelled, fairly triumphed.

Fritz was waiting for her.

Aimée knew nothing more, except that suddenly she raised her hand, and swung far out on the swaying bar, unfastened the hasp on which it hung.

And Fritz flew over.

She saw no more; there was no scream. Only a sound as if a bag of sand had struck the floor.

For the fraction of a second Aimée waited on her swing: now she knew that death was a delight. She let go, screamed and plunged into the chasm below.

As if all bonds had burst, hundreds had fled in horror. Men leaped to the barriers and dashed off, women streamed through the aisles in flight. No one waited, everyone fled. The women screamed as if they were being stabbed.

Three physicians ran up, and knelt beside the bodies.

Then everything was still. As if they wished to hide, the performers crept into their dressing-rooms, shuddering at every sound.

An attendant whispered something to the physicians. The bodies were picked up and laid upon the same piece of canvas. Silently they were carried out, through the aisle, through the stable, where the horses became restless in the stalls. The artists followed, a queer procession of mourners, in the various costumes of the pantomime.

The big baggage van stood ready. Adolf got in and placed them on the floor, side by side in the dark, first Aimée, then his brother. How dully their hands dropped back to the floor of the baggage wagon.

Then the door was closed.

A woman shrieked, and rushing forward, clung to the wagon. It was Louise. They slowly carried her away.

Just then one of the waiters from the restaurant came running along the cold, bare hall, frightened, as if he had seen a ghost amid all this brightness.

He was calling for a doctor. A woman, he said, was lying in convulsions in the restaurant. One of the three physicians ran up, and a carriage was sent for. It drove up, with gorgeous escutcheons on the panels, and a lady was let out to it, supported by the physician.

Her equipage was forced to wait a moment. The narrow street was blocked by the big baggage van.

Then the equipage passed it and drove on.

In the street were bright lights and a great crowd. Two young men standing under a lantern. With happy watchful glances they surveyed the busy square. Two others walked up to them, and related the event. They cursed a little; all was described with much gesticulation. Then the two news-carriers moved on.

The first two gentlemen stood still. One of them struck the

paving stones with his stick.

"Well," he said, "mon dieu, les pauvres diables."

And forthwith, their eyes fixed on the milling crowd, they began to hum:

> *Amour, amour,*
> *Oh, bel oiseau,*
> *Chante, chante,*
> *Chante toujours.*

Their silver-headed canes gleamed. The young men sauntered away in their long coats.

> *Amour, amour,*
> *Oh, bel oiseau,*
> *Chante, chante,*
> *Chante toujours.*

THE END

VERY SHORT CLASSICS

This book is part of the 'Very Short Classics' series, a collection of short books from around the world and across the centuries, many of which are being made available as ebooks, and paperback, for the very first time.

Also available in the Very Short Classics series…

CHILDLESS by Ignát Herrmann

A classic Czech novella.

When Ivan Hron is expelled from university because of his political beliefs he is kicked out of the family home and disinherited by his father. He finds a job in Prague as a bank clerk, works hard and impresses his employers. Some years later, he is appointed manager.

Now a man of considerable means he is keen to get married and start a family. One summer holiday he meets Magdalena, a young woman from the country who is at the resort with her parents, and falls in love. But his proposal of marriage is refused.

Six months pass and Ivan hears that Magda's father has fallen upon hard times. He gets back in touch, repeats his proposal and this time is accepted. And although their union is seemingly a happy one, it remains childless, much to Ivan's distress.

One day, Ivan discovers a letter his wife has hidden from him. The contents shatter his illusions of their happy marriage and reveal secrets that challenge everything he has hoped for in life.

But his reaction will surprise those around him and, quite possibly, the reader too.

Childless is a short novella by a revered Czech writer whose work is little-known in English. Its forward-thinking philosophy, way ahead of its time, makes it a story that deserves a modern readership.

SOUVENIRS OF FRANCE by Rudyard Kipling

'Sixty pages… of memory, praise, nostalgia and gratitude' Julian Barnes

Rudyard Kipling's love affair with India is well-documented but his affection for France and its people is less well-known. It started at the age of twelve when he would regularly accompany his father to the Paris Exhibition of 1878, where the elder Kipling was in charge of the Indian Section of Arts and Manufactures. Young Rudyard would be sent off in the morning with two francs in his pocket and instructions to stay out of trouble. He would spend his money on 'satisfying déjeuners' and 'celestial gingerbreads' as well as frequent trips up inside the head of the Statue of Liberty, then part of the Exhibition prior to being shipped to Ellis Island.

He returned to France a decade later, as a young man, and then regularly in the years that followed, sometimes for pleasure, sometimes on business – such as when working for the British Imperial War Graves Commission. He was a frequent visitor for the rest of his life.

Souvenirs of France was originally published in 1933, and was one of the last of Kipling's books to appear during his lifetime. It is a very personal and fascinating portrait of a great writer and of a country that had a special place in his heart.

This edition first published by Very Short Classics 2018

Copyright © Very Short Classics 2018

All rights reserved. No part of this publication may be reproduced, stored or transmitted in any form or by any means, electronic, mechanical, photocopying, recording, scanning, or otherwise without written permission from the publisher. It is illegal to copy this book, post it to a website, or distribute it by any other means without permission.

Originally published in English by William Heinemann in 1927.

Translation by Marie Ottilie Heyl

ISBN: 9798655364653

Printed in Poland
by Amazon Fulfillment
Poland Sp. z o.o., Wrocław